Miserable in Montana

Cheryl Wright

Copyright

Miserable in Montana

Table of Contents

Dedication

To Margaret Tanner, my very dear friend and fellow author, for her enduring encouragement and friendship.

To Alan, my husband of over forty-six years, who has been a relentless supporter of my writing and dreams for many years.

To Virginia McKevitt, cover artist and friend, who always creates the most amazing covers for my books.

To You, my wonderful readers, who encourage me to continue writing these stories. It is such a joy knowing so many of you enjoy reading my stories as much as I love writing them for you.

Chapter One

Harrietville, Montana – 1880

"Wait up, Marigold," Luke Jensen called. "Wait up!" he shouted with annoyance as she continued to walk away from him.

Marigold Davis continued her quest toward home, her step a little quicker than before. If there was one thing Ma drummed into her, it was to avoid Luke Jensen at all costs. After all, he was one of the bad boys in town, and she must never hang around his sort.

Despite her resistance, Luke quickly caught up, his long legs sure to be the reason. She dared not look at him but instead, glanced sideways. He was easy on the eyes, and no matter what Ma said, she didn't mind stealing a glance or two. He suddenly stepped in front of her, running his hands through his slicked back hair, glistening in the sunlight.

"You need to move, Luke," she said, looking him up and down. Marigold suddenly felt warm all over.

Instead he stood grinning down at her, and she melted. He always did make her feel this way, ever since they met when she was fifteen years old and was working part time in the Mercantile. She guessed Luke went there to see her, because he never bought much, only a few sweets. Sometimes he just hung around.

"You look beautiful today, Marigold," he said, his face softening. "That hat looks real pretty on you."

Did that mean she didn't look pretty without the hat? She glared at him.

"I mean…" He ran his fingers through his hair again. "I didn't mean nothing bad by it. You know that."

He studied her with those dreamy chocolate colored eyes, like maybe he wasn't sure she did know what he meant. "Do I?" She was teasing him now. It was a cat and mouse game they'd often played. Luke was well aware of her mother's opinion of him. *Gutter trash*, that's what Ma always said, and maybe it was true, maybe it wasn't. Either way, it wasn't Luke's fault. He had no choice in what life dished out to him.

Suddenly, he changed tack. "Come to the dance with me Saturday night?"

It was her turn to study him. He sure was good looking, and it would feel mighty fine to arrive at the dance on his strong arm. *What would it be like to be held by him as they danced?*

"Marigold? Are you even listening to me?" He was in front of her again, this time glaring at her. At least she thought he was. The expression came and went in a heartbeat.

"I'll think about it," she said as she came back to the present. The moment the words were out, she wished them gone. Ma would never allow it, and Marigold would never think of betraying her. As fragile as she was, Ma worked hard to support them both by doing cleaning jobs. Marigold helped with the household income by working at the Mercantile when there was work available. It was the best she could manage. Even then she was certain she had that job out of pity. Sometimes it riled her, but mostly she was grateful her boss was looking out for her.

"So what do you say?" He bent down to her height and stared right into her eyes. They were face to face, and their lips were oh so close. It was her undoing.

"Oh for goodness sakes," she said breathlessly. "If I say yes will you leave me alone?"

He fist pumped the air and picked her up, spinning her around until she begged him to stop. He placed her gently back on the sidewalk, and caught her in his arms when she went off balance. She wondered if he'd done it on purpose, so he could hold her.

She breathed in his cologne, not able to help herself, then relaxed into him. Luke pulled her closer still, and it felt nice. She felt protected in his arms, and she didn't want him to let go.

Then she remembered her mother's words and pulled out of his grip. *He'll pull you down to his level, that one*, Ma had said. But Luke wasn't like that. Luke was… special.

"Where are you off to?" Ma called from her bed. She was ailing tonight and Marigold almost called off her plans to go to the dance with Luke.

"I'm not going, Ma," she called back. "I'll stay home and look after you." Luke would be disappointed for sure, and so would Marigold. Ma had done so much for her over the years, and it was time to pay her back, even if it was only by being on hand in case she needed something.

She spun around at the shuffling noise behind her. "Ma! What are you doing out of bed? You'll catch a chill." She quickly closed the distance between them and led her mother back to bed. It was the middle of winter, and Ma was already unwell. She didn't need a chill to make things worse.

As she lay Ma down in the crumpled bed, she noticed the fire had almost burned out. "Let me fix that fire before I do anything else." She fiddled with the fire and got it going, careful not to soil her one and only party gown.

"You going to the dance?" Ma's shaky voice made her heart break in two.

She glanced over her shoulder. "No Ma. I'm staying home tonight. There will be other dances." As the flames licked at the twigs and logs, Marigold stood.

Ma began to sit up, and slid her legs out of the bed. "You need to get back into bed," Marigold admonished her mother. She lay back down immediately, a frown on her face. Her daughter lifted her legs and tucked them under the blankets.

"I'll only stay in bed if you go to the dance," she said, her voice low. "Which young man are you going with?"

Marigold crossed her fingers behind her back. If Ma knew she was going with Luke, she'd explode. But she wasn't really going with him – she was making her own way to the dance. "I'm going alone," she said, knowing she was pushing the truth with that statement.

Ma stared at her, then motioned her closer. She kissed her only child's cheek. "Enjoy yourself," she said, then closed her eyes as if dismissing further discussion.

As she left the room, Marigold felt more than a little guilty. She had lied to Ma by omission. Sure she was meeting Luke at the dance, but in truth, she would be with him throughout the night. Why Ma hated Luke's family she would never know. Not that she knew a lot about them – it wasn't a subject that had ever been discussed. Even when Pa was alive any talk of the Jensen's was shut down.

She returned to her bedroom in the loft and finished preparing for the dance. Her party gown was a hand-me-down from cousin Mary, but it was still a favorite amongst the few gowns she owned. They'd never had much money, even when Pa was alive, but it wasn't something Marigold liked to dwell on. *That sort of thing never helped no-one*, Ma always said, and she was right.

They had food on the table, a roof over their heads, and clothes to wear. It would be far easier though, if Marigold managed to find a job that was more than just a few hours a couple of days a week.

She fashioned her hair so it hung down around her shoulders, and placed her most favorite hat on her head. The colors matched her gown, and the flowers enhanced her face. At least she thought so. What Luke would think was an entirely different thing.

Marigold pulled on her white gloves, and put on her thick coat. It had definitely seen better days, but the best she had.

She was ready to leave but would say goodbye to Ma first. She stood in the doorway watching Ma sleep. She watched her chest go up and down, convinced she was still alive. If she was dying, would Ma even tell her? She thought not.

Satisfied her mother was still alive, she quietly left the room and opened the front door. She locked it behind her then headed down the short path to the street. As she turned the corner, she saw the silhouette of a man on the corner. Right where she needed to go to get to the dance. It made her hesitate.

She was about to cross the road to avoid him when he hurried toward her. Her heart thundered in her chest. "Marigold," he called out. "Where are you going?"

She sighed in relief at the sound of Luke's voice. "What are you doing here," she asked firmly. "I said I'd meet you there." Annoyance filled her, but she was also grateful it was him.

He glanced about. "There was no way I was letting you walk there alone. Anyone could be lurking about."

That made her smile. "Like you, do you mean?"

Her words made her chuckle, and he joined in. "I guess so."

He offered her his arm, and she gladly took it. She might have been annoyed with him earlier, but now she was relieved. Luke was right – anyone could be lurking about. Especially on this side of town. It wasn't the safest place at night.

She glanced up at the handsome man escorting her to the dance, and a zing went through her. How long had she pined after Luke Jensen? It was over a decade now, but instead of silly teenagers, they were both adults. To her disgust, she still wanted him as much now as she did back then.

When they arrived at the hall, Luke pulled out two tickets and handed them over. The atmosphere was alive, and Marigold was glad Ma had pushed her into coming. Couples were on the dance floor, standing close to each other and swaying to the music. Streamers hung from the walls, giving the place a party feel.

"Come on," Luke said, helping her out of her threadbare coat and handing it over for safekeeping. "Let's dance."

She studied him. "We've just arrived." Despite her protests, he pulled her onto the dance floor and wrapped his arms around her. Marigold rested her head on his chest. She could hear his heart beating fast and steady, and wondered what he was thinking. He wasn't a teenager anymore, far from it, and she wondered if she was in his thoughts.

His arm wandered from around her back, to a little lower down. "Luke Jensen!" She pulled herself away from him in time to see him grin. "It is far from funny," she said, then stormed over to one of the chairs scattered about the room.

He didn't look the least bit guilty, in fact he looked rather elated. "If I promise to keep my hands to myself, will you come and dance with me again?" The grin was finally gone, but he still didn't look as though he regretted his actions. "Please?"

She waited for him to apologize, but the words never came. She truly believed he wasn't the least bit sorry. Deep down she felt delighted about what he'd done. It cemented what she'd always thought, that Luke had feelings for her.

On the other hand, he might just think she was an easy target. Now she wasn't sure whether she should be angry with him or not. But Luke wasn't the sort of person you could stay angry with for long.

The music stopped and she was suddenly disappointed. "Too late," she said quietly. Not that she would admit to enjoying being in his arms, but there would be other chances tonight. At least she hoped there would be.

Luke sat beside her and took her hand. His thumb caressed the back of her hand, and she wondered how many other women he'd done this same thing to. She glanced up to see him staring at her.

He brushed back a stray lock of her hair. "You are so beautiful, Marigold," he said quietly. "You always were." He reached out and his other thumb traced the lines of her lips.

Her heart rate kicked up and he continued to hold her hand. Without warning, the music started again. "Come on, let's dance," he said, pulling her onto the dance floor. She didn't refuse.

Once again he wrapped his arms around her and pulled her to him. "Keep your hands to yourself this time," she warned, and he grinned down at her.

"I'll try," he said. "But I'm not making any promises." She never tired of seeing that grin. When he grinned his dimples kicked in, and she always found them hard to resist. It reminded her of the time he'd pulled her behind the church hall away from everyone else, and kissed her.

She was sixteen and he was almost eighteen. He'd pinned her against the wall so she couldn't escape, then stared down into her eyes. She thought she was going to melt – to think that Luke Jensen had picked her out of all the girls in town. It was enough to make a young girl swoon. His arms went up around her back and he pulled her roughly to him, much how an inexperienced teenage boy would. Her heart had pounded. If Pa had found out, he would have belted the living daylights out of Luke. She was absolutely certain of it.

As she'd stared into his alluring brown eyes, Luke suddenly covered her mouth with his. He seemed to stay that way for ages, and she eventually had to pull back so she could breathe. Thinking about it now, he must have thought her the amateur she was. He'd stared down at her and grinned, then released her. Marigold ran away as fast as she could, never telling a soul about their encounter.

He'd pursued her ever since.

"This is nice," he said quietly, and she nodded in response. She didn't want to break the spell she was under. Instead she tightened her grip on him, and snuggled closer. "We should do this more often," he said, and she glanced up at him.

"It might be difficult," she whispered. "You know how Ma feels about you." Saying the words out loud filled her with sadness. She really liked Luke, despite his bad reputation, and would willingly spend more time with him. Upsetting Ma was the last thing she wanted to do.

She heard him sigh. "I don't know what I ever did to make your mother hate me," he said softly. "I'm not a bad person."

Marigold knew it was true. Luke was always gentle with her, if a little pushy. Despite that, this was the first time she'd agreed to go out with him, and she was so pleased that she had. She'd always worried what Ma would think, but she was a grown woman now – it was her choice entirely.

Chapter Two

Luke walked her right to her front door despite Marigold's protests. "What if Ma comes out," she whispered, not wanting to give them away.

Instead of waiting for an answer, she stared into his eyes, then leaned against him. Luke's hands made their way up her back where he caressed her. She sank into him.

His fingers were suddenly under her chin, coercing her to look up at him. Was he going to kiss her like he had all those years ago? She sure hoped so, but she worried what Ma would say if she found out.

She licked her lips and moments later he swooped on her lips. She felt herself melt against him like she had that day behind the church hall. For some strange reason she wanted to run away like she had back then. Luke's strong arms held her in place and all thoughts of running disappeared.

Every time she saw him it reminded her of that day. She'd dreamed of kissing him so many nights since, and now it was happening, she wasn't sure it was the right thing to do.

She heard herself quietly groan and opened her eyes. "I, I can't be doing this," she said quietly as she pushed him away. "What if Ma comes out?"

He grinned at her. "What if your Ma comes out? You are grown now, Marigold." He leaned in and gave her a quick kiss. "It's your choice who you go out with, not your Ma's." Luke was right, she knew he was, but she felt a certain loyalty to her mother, who had looked out for her all these years.

She stared up at him, and he licked his lips. "Marigold." His words came out on a breath, and he leaned in to kiss her again. She pushed him away from her, but he was too strong and pulled her closer.

Her heart pounded, not because she was worried he'd do something against her will, because she knew he wouldn't, but because of their closeness. She'd waited so long for this.

His hands were suddenly cupping her face, and he leaned into her. She tried to swallow, but her mouth was dry. He stood staring down at her as though waiting for her consent. She nodded and he kissed her.

Everything around her ceased to exist. Her heart pounded and a thrill ran through her. It was like fireworks going off inside her.

"Is that you out there, Marigold?"

She heard her Ma's voice moments before the door flew open, and they pulled apart. Luke stood planted to the ground. Irritation ran through her. "It's only me, Ma," she called hoping her mother would go away, but it was too late.

"You! What are you doing here, Luke Jensen?" Ma demanded. Marigold glanced up at him, her heart pounding.

"Good evening, Mrs Davis." He smiled at her as though his presence wasn't the worst thing that could happen. "I wanted to ensure Marigold arrived home safely. You can't trust anyone these days."

Ma stared at him, and not in a good way, then her face softened a little. "Thank you," she said, not sounding particularly grateful. Leaving the door wide open, she walked away, pulling her robe tightly around herself.

"Can I see you tomorrow?" Luke whispered.

She glanced back over her shoulder at him. "Won't you be working?" She watched as his shoulders stiffened, but had no idea why.

"I work nights," he said matter-of-factly. "Maybe we can take a stroll in the park? Can I pick you up at eleven?"

Should she? Marigold really wanted to say yes, but was torn between her own wants and her mother's feelings. He reached out and grasped her arm.

"It's just a walk in the park," he said, his eyes pleading with her.

She never could resist those eyes. "Alright, but I'll meet you there." She stared at him momentarily, daring him to refuse her request, but he said nothing. Marigold scurried inside, and closed the door behind her.

~*~

Luke checked his watch. Marigold was twenty minutes late. Was she even coming?

He willed his heart rate to slow down. Why was he so set on seeing her today?

He already knew the answer – he'd waited years for her, more than ten. He couldn't bear to have his heart broken yet again. And if she didn't show? He dare not even think about it, because if she didn't eventually turn up, he'd know she'd made her decision.

He got up from the wooden bench and began to pace the dirt path, then to try and distract himself he wandered down to the stream where a handful of ducks were enjoying the water. Not that it was very deep; ducks didn't need much water to swim. As long as they could kick their little legs they were happy.

"Luke!" He spun around at the sound of her voice, and his heart did a little flutter. He'd only seen her last night, so why did her presence make him feel so excited? Exhilarated.

"You made it. I thought you weren't coming." It was true, he'd been on the verge of leaving several times, but forced himself to stay. She'd never broken her word before and he had no reason to think she would this time.

"I'm really sorry," she said quietly. "Ma needed my help." She looked on the brink of tears, so he pulled her close and rubbed his hands across her back.

He stared into her sad face. Last night she'd been happy and had enjoyed their night together. Today she seemed the opposite. "Is there anything I can do to help?" He would help where he could, but figured Marigold would deny his offer anyway.

She shook her head. "Ma has worked so hard all her life, even when Pa was alive." She glanced up at him. "I think she's just plumb worn out."

Luke dearly wanted to tell her the truth, but it wasn't his story to tell. Besides, he risked losing her if he said anything. Making him out to be the bad guy when he was innocent. It was so unfair.

A tear rolled down her cheek and he gently brushed it away. "I wish I could do something to help. If I could get a better job, one with longer hours, and Ma could give up work."

He leaned down and kissed her forehead. "Try not to worry," he said gently. "I'm sure something will turn up."

She said nothing, but pulled out of his grip. He wanted to hold her longer, to comfort her, but he also didn't want her upset, and if she stayed in his arms any longer, he knew that's what would happen.

"Shall we visit the ducks?" he asked as she hooked her arm through his. "There are a few there, some ducklings too."

That seemed to brighten her up a bit, and she almost ran toward the stream. "I should have brought some bread," she said as they got closer to the edge of the stream.

He reached into his pocket, glad for his last minute idea to bring some along. "I have a few slices," he said, handing it over. Her face lit up with delight and she gently hugged him.

For the next few minutes they stood in silence as she threw bread to the ducks. They fluttered about, each trying to reach it before the others. When it was all gone, they continued on the pathway through the park. There were trees scattered about and a number of native bushes. Here and there beds of flowers could be found. It was a work-in-progress, and still needed quite a bit of work to make it palatable, but it was quiet and they had privacy away from prying eyes.

The last thing Luke wanted was for Maggie Davis to find out he was trying to court her daughter. The woman hated him with a vengeance. What happened to her husband was not his parent's fault, or indeed his fault, but Mrs Davis had never believed that, and likely never would.

Why should Marigold have to pay for the sins of her father? It was totally unfair.

He stared down into her face. Such beauty. He'd known when she was just a teenager she would be beautiful beyond his imagination, and he was right. Not only was she beautiful on the outside, but the inside as well. Marigold had always been such a sweet thing, and he'd regretting cornering her that day behind the church hall. Teenage shenanigans, brought about by hormones.

Still, he hadn't regretted kissing her, but for a moment he felt he'd frightened her. He would never do anything to harm her, not ever. Not that she'd known it or ever would, but he'd protected her back then. He'd looked out for her, and kept the scum of the earth gang boys away from his sweet Marigold.

He even had the scars to prove it.

"…long."

Luke's head shot up. What had he missed with his reminiscing? "Sorry, I was a million miles away. What did you say?"

She grinned at him, and it took all his resistance not to kiss her. "I said I have to work this afternoon. I can't stay too long." She looked far from happy about the prospect. "The little I earn isn't even enough to put food on the table."

He knew things were tight, but had no idea they were so bad, and his heart broke. A thought suddenly came to him. "What if I could get you a job? One with far more hours." He glanced down at her.

Her eyes opened wide. "Could you?" She sounded so excited, and looked happy too.

"You would have to work at night," he said quietly, not sure she would be interested. Now he was not so sure he should have even mentioned it. He knew she wouldn't take money from him, but he would gladly help her out.

"I am not that sort of girl, Luke Jensen!" she screamed at him, and pushed him away. She began to run from him and he grabbed her arm.

"Marigold," he said, lifting her chin with his fingers. "I know you would never do *that*." He leaned in and kissed her forehead. Perhaps he'd gone about this the wrong way. "On second thought, I have a friend who is looking for a reliable waitress. Local too," he said. Yes, that would be far better. "Do you think you could do that?"

She glared at him. "Are you sure that's all I'd have to do?" He felt hurt that she thought he would try to make her work as a soiled dove. He would never, especially not to sweet innocent Marigold. Besides, he wanted her for himself when she agreed to marry him.

His first suggestion of working for him would never work. Not that she knew that's what he was suggesting. It had far too many hurdles anyway. For one, how would Marigold get to and from work in another town? It would be a logistical nightmare.

He wished he'd never mentioned it. He should have simply asked her to marry him. That way he could supported her and Mrs Davis and no one would think anything about it. She would have no reason to complain then. Now it was too late. He'd already opened his mouth and couldn't take the words back.

Or could he?

"Why don't we get married?" he blurted out.

At first she stared at him, concern written all over her face. Then she burst out laughing. "You always were a joker," she said, but stopped laughing when he didn't join in.

"I wasn't joking," he said, his feelings hurt at her reaction. "I'm serious. That way you wouldn't need to work." He felt hollow. Had he just ruined his chances with Marigold? He certainly hoped not – he'd pined for her since their teenage years. "Your mother too. I would support you both once we married."

She stared at him. Oh, he knew the thoughts running through her head – her mother had taken care of that. Marigold thought he was the worst of the worst and was penniless. Mrs Davis couldn't be farther from the truth.

He reached out and held her by the waist. Touching her, even through her coat, sent a thrill down his spine. He wanted so much to hold her right now, but would she refuse his advances after what he'd just said?

She continued to study him. She was trying to decide if he was being serious or really was joking. "If you can get me the details of that waitress job, I'll look into it," she said, her voice shaking. Was she really going to ignore his proposal?

"Good. Have lunch with me tomorrow and I'll give you the information. Bunny's Café at noon?" He held his breath waiting for her response. Finally she nodded, and he walked her back home in silence.

What would Marigold say when she eventually found out where he worked? The business he owned. He'd deal with that when it happened.

Marigold was torn. She appreciated the paltry number of hours work she got each week, she really did, but desperately needed a job with longer hours and far better pay. She had never really enjoyed working there, but felt a certain loyalty to her boss. Besides, she badly needed the money.

Sure, he'd helped put money in the household pool, but it was never enough. Her poor worn out mother contributed the bulk of the household income, and even between them, it was never enough.

Ma had worked hard for as long as Marigold could remember. Scrubbing floors and doing laundry for well-to-do clients on the other side of town had run her into the ground. By the time Saturday night rolled around, Ma was far too tired to enjoy her life, and spent most of the time in bed trying to ease the pain of her body or simply sleeping. It broke Marigold's heart.

If *she* could get a full-time job that paid a decent wage, Ma could give up work. At her age, Ma shouldn't still be working, but refused to allow Marigold to take on the same sort of work, or even to take over from her.

Ma called it a form of slavery, said it had ruined her life. She was probably right.

"Marigold?" Her head shot up as Mrs Quinn stood impatiently at the counter with her purchases. "Did you even hear a word I said?" she snapped. Marigold hoped Mr Green didn't hear the retort. It could be the end of the handful of hours work she had each week. Her only savior would be if she managed to secure the waitressing job Luke had mentioned yesterday. He made it sound as though the job was hers if she wanted it, but that surely wasn't true.

Marigold brushed a nervous hand across her forehead. "Sorry, my mind was elsewhere." She smiled briefly at the customer and pulled out the account book, writing each item down carefully. "All done," she said when she'd finished entering each purchase. "Can I carry it out to the buggy for you?"

"Thank you, Marigold." Mrs Quinn was always polite but it was obvious the woman thought herself higher up the rung than Marigold, and it stung.

Once back inside, she tidied up the shelves to fill in the last fifteen minutes of her shift. Then she would head to the diner and have lunch with Luke. Her heart fluttered at the thought of seeing him again. Not that she'd told Ma – she was at work, so would never find out.

The notion caused guilty pangs. She would be off galivanting about with Luke Jensen having a lovely lunch, while Ma slaved away at the Hannigan's mansion, scrubbing their floors. Her only saving grace was the fact she would find out about the waitressing job Luke had told her about.

She pulled off her apron and hung it behind the door.

Mr Green came out of the storeroom and headed toward the cash register. He pulled out a few notes, handing them to her. "I'm sorry, Marigold," he said quietly. "I'm afraid today was your last shift."

Her head shot up, and she swallowed hard, trying to force back her emotions. "Oh, Mr Green," she said shakily. "Did I do something wrong?"

He reached into the register and handed her some more notes. "Take this as a small bonus," he said gently. "Business isn't what it used to be, and I can no longer justify paying anyone. I'm really sorry, Marigold. I know you need the money."

She nodded, but was feeling far too emotional to say much. "Thank you," she finally managed, and pulled on her coat and gloves, then left. Her only hope was that Luke hadn't been leading her on. Despite him having a reputation as a no-hoper, he'd never proven to be unreliable for as long as she'd known him.

"There you are," he said, leaping toward her as she approached the diner. "I was beginning to worry." He stared at her. "Are you alright? You don't look your usually bubbly self."

She couldn't bear to look at him and admit what happened, so stared to the ground instead. "I lost my job. Mr Green says he can't afford to pay me any longer."

"That's great," Luke said, then slipped his arm around her waist.

She glared at him. "Great? Did you even hear what I said?" Her heart thudded. If the proposed job didn't work out, she would be in real strife, and would have to take on whatever came along despite her mother's protests.

"Trust me," he said, and lifted her chin with his gloved fingers, but it was little consolation. "Let's go inside out of the cold." He led her into the cozy diner where they sat at a small table close to the fire. He helped Marigold out of her coat, and she pulled off her gloves. The warmth of the fire enveloped her almost immediately.

A middle-aged woman approached their table. "Hello Luke," she said as she placed a bottle of water on the table, along with two glasses. "Who's your friend," the other woman asked. She placed a glass in front of each of them, and poured out the water.

"Barbara West," he said, "But everyone calls her Bunny. This is Marigold Davis."

"Pleased to meet you Marigold." The woman looked tired, and as Marigold looked around, realized there were no other staff.

"You too," Marigold said. "You here alone?" she asked.

"For now. What can I get you?" She handed them each a menu, and Marigold's eyes skimmed it. There wasn't much on the menu, but if Bunny was handling the entire place alone, it was no wonder.

"The hearty soup looks good. I'll have that please," Marigold said before she could change her mind.

"Make it two thanks Bunny."

More customers came through the door and Bunny guided them to a table. She disappeared into the kitchen and came out a short time later with their order on a small wooden tray. She left a plate of sliced bread and some butter in the center of the table. "It smells delicious, thank you," Marigold said as she leaned in to get the full aroma of the soup.

"The food is always wonderful here," Luke told her. "Eat up," he said, indicating her food.

It was a busy diner, and Marigold spent a lot of her time watching Bunny trying to balance between seating customers and serving the food. "How does she even do it?" she asked her luncheon companion.

He grimaced. "With great difficulty. What do you think of the food?"

She studied him, then looked down into her empty bowl. "It was delicious." She was far too distracted by Bunny's situation to think too much about the now non-existent food. "What about yours?" She was simply being polite, and was certain Luke knew it.

"Always," he said, then reached across the table to cover her hand. "About that waitressing job I told you about," he said, keeping his voice low. "Are you still interested?"

"Definitely," she said. "Especially now that I don't have a job to go back to."

His head shot up and he nodded. She wasn't sure what was going on and followed the direction he was looking. As she turned, she saw a smile cross Bunny's face, then a look of relief. The older woman walked over to their table.

"The job is yours if you want it." Bunny stared down at Marigold, her eyes begging her to say yes. "You will start at seven, and finish at three, six days a week. You can have extra shifts if you want them. The evening meal is always busy."

Marigold sat in stunned silence. She had not been asked to prove her skills as a waïtress. Indeed, she had not been asked to prove anything.

"The job is mine?" Her eyes filled with tears and she fought back the emotion of knowing she finally had a proper job and Ma could retire. Luke squeezed her hand.

"It really is," he said gently, then reached out and wiped a stray tear away.

"Can you start tomorrow? I can really do with the help, as you can see."

Bunny's words pulled her out of her emotions. She glanced about. By now the place was almost full, and the poor woman looked exhausted. "No, I can't," she said, then suddenly stood. "You need help right now."

Bunny wore a grin from ear to ear, and she suddenly moved forward and hugged Marigold tightly. "I can see we're going to get along fine," she said, then took Marigold's hand and led her into the kitchen. Marigold glanced back over her shoulder to see a satisfied smile on Luke's face.

Chapter Three

"Don't argue, Ma," Marigold said firmly. "I've already started at my new job, and it pays far more than what we have earned between us in the past."

Ma stared at her. "How can that be?" She shook her head in disbelief.

"Well… it's a busy café, and I'll be working six days a week." She shrugged. She hadn't really thought about the money part before, and just accepted it was good. "The owner is lovely and it's permanent, so no worrying about losing my hours.

She said she'll teach me to cook when she has the time. Fancy stuff too."

Taking a sip of her coffee, Ma shook her head. "It sounds good, but how do we know we can trust her? What if I quit my job, meagre as it is, and yours falls through? What then?"

Marigold didn't know what to say to that. The last thing she could tell Ma was that Luke had arranged the job for her. He'd known Bunny for some years he'd said, and she'd been desperate for help after her waitress left to get married. That was over a month ago, and it showed. Poor Bunny looked beyond exhausted. She had that haunted look Ma always wore.

Marigold had needed little instruction on how to serve the customers and had seen the expression of relief on the other woman's face from the moment she had donned the apron provided. She'd worked hard for the rest of the day, and stayed until the doors were locked for the evening.

Bunny had even given her some leftover food to take home.

"These rolls are delicious," Ma said, wiping butter from her mouth. "How much you will get to bring home?"

"We'll share the leftovers between us, Bunny said." Marigold knew Ma would be thinking about the savings for food as well as the money her daughter would be earning. It was a win all round. "It will depend on how busy the café is each day."

Ma nodded as she took another mouthful. "As long as you're certain, I won't go back to my back-breaking job."

Marigold was happy with the turn of events. Ma had been paid today, so she had no need to go back. She'd been treated so badly for many years that she owed nothing to anyone. All she had to do now was sit back and enjoy the rest of her life. Warmth spread through Marigold that she was finally able to do something to give back to her mother.

She sliced up the leftover apple pie Bunny had given her. There was just enough for a good-sized piece each. "Oooh, this is decadent," Ma said as she ate a spoonful of pie. "If they teach you to cook like this, you'll be able to snap yourself up a good husband." She stared up at Marigold. They'd talked about the subject a lot. If she found someone she loved, then she'd marry them if they asked. But eligible bachelors were hard to find around here. Well-to-do bachelors were even more difficult to find for someone like her.

As she remembered Luke's proposal, warmth filled her because she had a soft spot for him, but knew she shouldn't take much notice of that. He was trying to get her out of a bad situation. He'd made up for his silliness by arranging this job for her. The best part being it was in walking distance. It wasn't pitch black when she had to come home, so that worked out well.

Still, being married to Luke could be... adventurous. Ma insisted he was a classic bad boy who lived on the wrong side of town. She seemed to forget *they* lived on the wrong side of town. Luke still lived in his parents' home where houses were far larger and much more expensive. Ma's house was a dollhouse in comparison. When his parents had passed on, Luke inherited the house. At least that's what she'd heard. She and Luke had been forced apart long ago, so she really didn't know him anymore.

Marigold had barely seen him since that kiss behind the church hall. After Pa died, Ma forbid her from seeing him ever again. Back then she was just a teenager, but now she was an adult, it was her choice who she did and didn't see. Her fingers suddenly flew to her lips at the thought of Luke's lips on hers. They tingled as though he'd kissed her only moments ago.

She had to forget Luke. He wasn't her type.

"If you had a husband," Ma said slowly, "You wouldn't need to work." She studied her and stared at Marigold through tiny slits. "At least if you picked wisely and he could support you." She reached out and covered her daughter's hand.

"You mean keep away from Luke, Ma?" Marigold pulled her hand back, and Ma stared at her.

"He's gutter trash," she spat, but she'd never explained why she thought that way.

Licking her lips, Marigold thought carefully about her next words. "He got me that waitressing job. We owe him a lot."

"Gutter trash!" Ma spat again, then pushed back her chair and shuffled out of the room leaving Marigold to stare after her.

Luke lay in bed, his hands behind his head, staring up at the ceiling.

Last night he'd had the best sleep. He had long worried about Marigold. Even when she was a slip of a girl and he wasn't much older, he'd worried. He'd overheard far too many conversations his parents had, thinking he was out of earshot, but he wasn't. When it came to Marigold, he was all ears.

He'd known from his early teenage years her father wasn't all he made out to be. The moment he was old enough, Luke was forced to work in his parent's business. Back then it was a terrible place. His mother tried to keep him away from the worst of it, but Pa said he needed to grow up and be a man. He was put to work in the kitchen to begin with, and worked his way up from there.

His utter distaste at the soiled doves working in their saloon did not sit well with Pa. Luke had earned many a clip around the ear because of it. Not that he disrespected the women, he would never do that. No, his aversion was focused on his father for forcing them into that situation. If they wanted to leave, they had to pay a large penalty. The vast majority did not have the money to buy their way out of their enforced situation.

There were still soiled doves working at his establishment, but none were there by force. They came voluntarily, and were free to leave whenever they wished. They were also paid extremely well for their services.

Luke was not a cruel man, and he had proven it time and again.

He'd first known Marigold's father had a gambling problem when he'd been thrown out of the saloon. It was that or face the wrath of the other gamblers. The man was relentless, he came back night after night. Luke knew money was tight in the Davis household, because Marigold had told him several times in her own innocent way. Even if she'd said nothing, he would have known. The poor girl was forced to wear hand-me-downs from distant cousins, and sometimes neighbors would even help out. It wasn't hard to be aware of their terrible situation.

He couldn't help her without admitting he knew what was going on, but as the years rolled by, it became apparent she had no idea of her father's sins. Including the fact he used the services of those soiled doves from time to time. Money that should have been used to put food on the table.

"Poor Marigold," he said out loud, and unable to sleep any longer, sat on the side of the bed. It was a little after seven in the morning, a time he'd prefer to be sleeping since he always worked into the early hours. Tossing and turning night after night didn't help his disposition, but today he felt a little more content. Since he'd hooked up with Marigold again, he had been in a better frame of mind, but still worried.

The fact he'd arranged a permanent position for Marigold was a big part of that. This job paid far better than she'd get elsewhere. His one hope was she would never find out he owned her new place of employment. It was a secret he'd managed to keep for many years.

He shuffled out the kitchen and filled the woodstove with newspaper and wood, then put the kettle on to boil. He didn't know why he bothered. Eating most of his meals at the café meant he didn't need to cook for himself. If he had a wife, they'd likely eat at home, but he didn't feel so lonely when he was surrounded by customers. Would she become suspicious when he was there twice a day? He hoped not.

He'd decided to walk Marigold to work for her first day. Although technically, yesterday was her first day. He couldn't have been more proud when she'd stood and followed Bunny into the kitchen to help immediately. That was just like her, thinking of others before herself.

He went to the bathroom and threw cold water into his face. He'd only managed a few hours sleep last night, but it was the deepest of sleeps, and he felt more refreshed than he had for ages.

The kettle had boiled by the time he returned to the kitchen. Luke glanced at his watch; he still had time to enjoy a leisurely mug of coffee before meeting up with Marigold. Not that she knew it, and would probably throw a fit when he turned up at her house. Especially if her Ma was up and about.

Now he needed to work on the old lady and get her to stop seeing him as the enemy. Until he managed that, he had no chance in marrying her daughter.

Marigold scoffed down the last of her breakfast, happy in the fact Ma was still sound asleep. She deserved a sleep in; she'd been getting up at the crack of dawn for as long as Marigold could remember.

She threw back the last of her coffee, then headed to the bathroom to brush and style her hair. Soon she'd be off to her new job. A little early perhaps, but rather that than late. Especially on her first day.

She fashioned her hair into a tight bun, and pulled her bonnet onto her head. She far preferred hats, but Ma constantly told her it wasn't the done thing. That the more refined young women wore bonnets. Marigold did not consider herself a refined woman – far from it.

If anyone could be considered gutter trash, it was Marigold, and certainly not Luke. She looked down at her worn gown with the small holes showing parts of her underskirts. With her first pay, she would rectify that. Of course she wouldn't go overboard, but with the money she was getting now, she could afford to buy two new day gowns to wear to work.

The last thing Bunny needed was for customers to be commenting on her state of dress. That would never do, and might even cause her to lose her job. Marigold swallowed. She couldn't afford for that to happen. She'd go out and buy the new gowns now if the funds were available, but until she was paid, they were still living on Ma's meagre payout from yesterday and the little she'd received from Mr Green at the Mercantile.

That said, she was very grateful for the small bonus he'd given her. It was barely enough to cover the cost of a few night's meals for the pair, but she was still thankful. He didn't have to do it, but Marigold knew it came from guilt on his part.

Pulling on her boots, she was finally ready. She reached for her coat, pulled on her gloves, and opened the front door, and there stood Luke Jensen. "What are you doing here?" she asked him, not entirely unhappy to see him. He silently helped her into her coat, his fingers rubbing over the material. She knew what he was thinking, and he was right. The coat needed replacing, but she didn't have the money for that. Not yet anyway. Perhaps in a few weeks. By then she would really need it as they'd be in the midst of winter, and the chill of the wind would go right to her bones.

He lifted his eyes from her coat and smiled. "I thought I'd walk you to work. I couldn't sleep anyway."

She couldn't help but grin. Luke Jensen got out of his warm bed to walk her to work. It didn't get any better than that. "Thank you, Luke. I appreciate it."

She quietly pulled the door closed behind her, happy in the knowledge her mother would have a far easier day today. It was her turn to bring in the money, and Marigold was more than happy to do so.

Luke slipped his gloved hand into hers, and she stared down at their entwined hands. "That's a bit forward of you, Luke Jensen," she said, but she didn't think for one minute he would pull his hand away, which he did. "I was only joking," she said, somewhat annoyed at the result. It felt good when he held her hand. Not as good as when he held her at the park – that was the best thing ever, and she would not complain if he did it again.

He slipped his hand back into hers, and Marigold was once again happy.

As they approached the café, they could see Bunny unlocking the front door from inside. She arrived far earlier to get started on the cooking, and Marigold felt bad. The other woman insisted it was not an issue since there were no customers there that early.

"Thanks for walking with me, Luke, but I have to start work now." He held the door open for her, then followed her inside. "What are you doing?" she asked when he sat down at one of the tables nearest the fire.

"I'm staying for breakfast," he said with a grin. "I come here for breakfast every day. Normally I'm not quite this early."

Her heart fluttered. She would get to see Luke every working day? She wasn't sure how she felt about that. More importantly, what would Ma say if she found out?

"In that case," she said, passing a menu over, "I'll get your coffee while you decide what you're having." She turned to go and make coffee, but he grabbed her hand and pulled her back.

"If I had the choice," he said as he looked her up and down, "I'd have you." She felt the heat travel from her neck all the way up her face. Oh my! Ma was right, Luke definitely *was* a bad boy!

He sighed. "Since I can't, then I'll have bacon and eggs with sausages and toast."

She backed up and scurried to the small nook next to the kitchen where the coffee was kept. She glanced across to where he sat to see him still grinning at her. Marigold busied herself making the first pot of coffee for the day – it gave her time to recover from Luke's risqué comment. The moment the coffee was ready, she returned with an empty mug and a pot of coffee. "Your food won't be long," she said, then turned to leave.

"Stay," he demanded, but she ignored him and scurried back to the coffee nook where she leaned against the wall in relief. Luke would wear her down if she wasn't careful, and that was the last thing she needed.

Soon his breakfast was cooked and she carried it out to him. "Sit down and talk to me," he said nonchalantly, as if it was normal for a waitress to sit with her customers.

She shook her head. "I can't, Luke. I have other customers to look after." It was true. By this time the café had filled up. There was now only one empty table, and another customer was about to enter. She rushed over and led the well-dressed gent to the table, then scampered off to get coffee for him.

The entire time she felt Luke's eyes burn through her. By the time she'd served the customer his coffee, it was time to deliver food to another table. She'd never been so busy in her life, but Marigold was enjoying her new job. Customers were constantly coming and going, and she barely got to take a breather, but she liked it. They all seemed nice, and no one had been nasty or spiteful, unlike at the Mercantile.

She guessed the quality of the clientele was consistent with the quality of the food and the prices. It was not cheap to eat here, but Bunny's cooking was top notch. Besides, most of the customers appeared to be business men going by their attire. Even Luke dressed like a businessman. But truth be known, Marigold had no idea what sort of work he did. She was certain Ma must know, but all she could get out of her was that he was *gutter trash*. That was far from fair.

Right now she didn't want to ask him what he did, but she would ask when it seemed appropriate. She recalled his parents owned a business out of town, something Ma didn't approve of. But she was only a teenager back then, and didn't take much notice. She had no idea if that business was even still going, let alone if Luke had inherited it.

The whole situation piqued her interest but it was a question for another day.

Luke finally stood as though he was leaving, and Marigold hurried over to clean up his table. He reached for her hand and covered it, causing her to leave the soiled dishes right where they were. Then he pulled her close and hugged her. "Luke!" she admonished him. "Remember where you are!" She was beyond annoyed with him, and tried to pull out of his arms, so he dragged her into the kitchen.

Bunny glanced up from her cooking and grinned. She didn't blink an eye. Was this normal practice for Luke to drag a woman into the kitchen to try and ravish her? A shudder went through her, and Marigold shoved him away. When she stared into his face, he looked hurt.

She was the one who should be hurt, not Luke. She wasn't that kind of girl, and was devastated he thought she was. She took a deep breath and let it out in a shudder. "What do you think you're doing, Luke?" she asked in a whisper.

He dared to laugh. "Bunny doesn't mind, do you?" The other woman simply shrugged her shoulders and went back to her cooking.

At that, he pulled her close again. This time he stole a kiss. She had to admit it felt nice to have Luke kiss her, but she had to wonder where else those lips had been. If he was truly as bad as her mother insisted, how many other girls had he kissed?

She shoved him away again. The last thing Marigold needed was to fall in love with bad boy Luke Jensen.

She was very afraid she was already half way there.

Chapter Four

Marigold had been at her new job nearly three weeks now, and Luke had walked her there each morning. He'd stayed for coffee and breakfast, then left after the reading the newspaper, which he left for other customers to enjoy.

He returned every day for a rather large luncheon, then left again. Working through the night had to be difficult, and he rarely had time to stop and eat, he'd said. That was the reason he came to the café for two large meals each day. That way he was sure to eat well and have enough food to sustain him.

They spent every Sunday together, first going to church together, then taking a stroll afterwards. Ma refused to attend church with them, and made her own way there. Being stubborn as she was, Ma sat as far away from Luke as she could get.

Luke wasn't a bad person, despite what Ma said, and Marigold wished she would see Luke for who he really was.

Marigold cleaned down the tables that had been recently vacated, and looked up as the door to the café opened.

Luke Jensen stood in the doorway holding a box. He glanced at her and grinned, and her heart fluttered. He only had to be in the same room and Marigold was flooded with warmth.

He was far too early for lunch, and the café was near to empty at this time of the day. It gave her time to ensure all the tables and chairs were thoroughly cleaned, replenish the sugar, and help Bunny with the dishes.

There had even been a few cooking lessons, which she rejoiced in. She'd been cooking since she was old enough to avoid being burned by the stove, but only basic meals. Never anything fancy. Bunny was teaching her to bake bread and rolls, pies, and desserts. Soon she would learn to make muffins and cookies.

One day she might even take over the café, Bunny had said. "You're hardly older than me," Marigold scoffed, but the other woman insisted.

Luke came up behind her as Marigold finished cleaning down the table. "You're early," she said as she grinned. She felt Luke's arm wrap around her waist and a shiver went through her. "Behave yourself," she whispered fiercely as she straightened up. She glanced about, but the few customers there for an early lunch were engrossed in their meals or reading the newspaper.

He took advantage and pulled her close. Marigold knew she shouldn't, but melted into him. The more she saw him, the more she wanted to spend time with Luke. Despite everything he'd done for them, Ma still hated him with a passion.

Marigold couldn't understand it. What had Luke Jensen or his parents ever done to Ma to cause all this hatred?

Her heart fluttered as he brought his head closer to hers. He was going to kiss her, right here in the middle of the café. At least she thought he was. She glanced up into his face. He was grinning at her, daring her to turn away from him. What a cheeky devil he could be at times!

She lifted her hand and placed her fingers across his lips, blocking his access to her.

He frowned, then gently pulled her fingers away, encasing them in his hand. Stealing a kiss, he held her tightly. "I have a something for you," he said quietly, then pulled her into the coffee nook.

"For me?" She couldn't have been more surprised. "Don't go wasting your money on the likes of me, Luke Jensen," she said quietly. "I'm sure you've better things to spend your hard-earned cash on."

Ignoring her words, he pushed the fancy box toward her. "It's never a waste spending on you, Marigold," he whispered in her ear. She felt his warm breath on her neck, and a shiver went through her. "Go on, open it," he said impatiently.

She looked over the elegant box – it looked far too expensive. She glanced up at him but he motioned for her to open it. She lifted it up to have a better look. In small gold letters on the side were the words, *Honey Blossom Boutique*. Marigold couldn't believe her eyes. It was the most expensive and exclusive store around, and never in her wildest dreams did she think she'd ever receive a gift from there.

She shook herself mentally. It was a box. Merely a box, and that didn't mean what was inside was from that store.

"Are you ever going to open your gift?" Luke asked impatiently. He reached across and flipped open the lid. Marigold stared down inside it for what seemed forever. She reached out and ran her fingers across it, stroking it back and forth and taking in the luxury of it. Glancing up at Luke, she didn't know what to say. For once in her life, she was totally speechless.

He sighed, then reached in and pulled out the item of her consternation. Luke had bought a new coat for her. Not just any coat, it was thick, it was luxurious, and it was the most glorious scarlet-coloured coat she'd ever seen. The label proved what she'd tried to deny – it said *Honey Blossom Boutique*. Her eyes filled with tears.

"You did this for me?" She rested her head against his chest. What a good friend Luke was, always looking out for her.

"The days are getting colder. You can't keep wearing that rag you have now."

Her elation turned to...she didn't know what. Anger? Resentment? Embarrassment? Perhaps a combination of all three. Her joy suddenly disappeared and she threw the coat back at him. "I don't want it," she ground out, then tried to get away, but he pulled her back.

He stared down into her face, his regret evident. "I'm sorry," he said quietly. "I didn't mean to upset you. It came out all wrong."

"It certainly did." She was still angry with him, but more than that, she was hurt to think he thought her clothes were rags.

"Can we start over?" he asked, still staring into her face. "It was meant to be something special, not something that tore us apart."

Without waiting for an answer, he pushed the luxurious coat back into her hands, then watched her every move as she rubbed her cheek against its softness. "Its beautiful, Luke, but I can't accept it. What would people think?"

He helped her into the coat. "Honestly, I don't care what people think. You're my girl and I'm entitled to buy you a gift."

His girl? Since when? At no time did she agree to be Luke's girl. If word got out, and Ma heard about it, there would be hell to pay.

As though he hadn't said anything untoward, Luke stood back and looked her up and down. "The size looks right. What do you think, Bunny?"

He stood aside for the cook to look it over. Her eyes opened wide when she saw the gift, then quirked an eyebrow at him. None of it went unnoticed by Marigold.

"It's beautiful, and the fit appears to be perfect." She moved back into the kitchen to her cooking.

The door to the café opened, and customers began to stream in for their noon meal. "I have to go," Marigold said. "Thank you," she added, then leaned forward and stole a quick kiss.

Luke helped her out of the coat. "Make sure you wear this home tonight," he said as she walked away from him and toward the customers. "It's already quite chilly in the evenings."

Marigold had a lot to think about, including whether or not she wanted to be Luke's girl. Her biggest worry was what Ma would say about her stepping out with one of the bad boys in town.

It was a busy afternoon, and Marigold flopped down into a chair the moment the last customer left.

"Can you believe how busy it was today?" she asked Bunny as she locked the door behind their last customer.

Bunny stared as Marigold cleaned down the tables ready for the morning when it would start all over again. Finally she shook her head. "I really can't. It's not like we're in the middle of town. People have to go out of their way to come here."

Marigold glanced up from what she was doing. "Word gets around. When people get good food, they tell others."

"We're far too expensive," Bunny said. "I keep telling Luke…" She suddenly stopped talking, her eyes wide.

"Why would you discuss it with Luke?" Marigold was totally confused. Bunny owned the café so why would she care what Luke thought?

Bunny worried her bottom lip, as though contemplating her next words. "Luke has been a good friend over the years. He, uh, he helped me out when I needed it."

Marigold stared at the other woman for a long moment, then nodded. That made perfect sense. Luke was always helping someone out of a bind.

She watched as the heat traveled up Bunny's face. Why would she be embarrassed? Everyone needed help at some point in their lives. Luke was in the right place at the right time for Marigold. If it wasn't for him, Ma would still be scrubbing floors on her hands and knees, and they'd still be living on the edge of poverty.

"Luke's great like that," Marigold said, trying to console the other woman and quell her embarrassment. "As you know, he helped me get this job. I don't know what I would have done without him."

Bunny nodded then headed back to the kitchen. "I have some extra rolls and more than enough beef and vegetable stew for your supper tonight if you'd like it," she called out.

Finished with the cleaning, Marigold wandered into the large kitchen. "That would be wonderful. Thank you, Bunny," she said. "I don't have anything planned for tonight. I told Ma to leave it to me." She felt a tad guilty, but since starting work at the café, she'd instructed Ma not to cook. That way if food was offered, they'd save money on their evening meal.

With the stipend she was being paid by Bunny, their lives were far easier, and they no longer had to skimp on everything. Old habits were hard to kick, and both Marigold and Ma found themselves acting as though things were like before.

Besides, the food was wonderful. Better than anything Marigold could make herself, and if they didn't take it home, it would go in the garbage. That would be a total waste, and she'd hate to see it happen. "Thank you," she said, as Bunny passed over a large shopping bag. Inside was a sealed bowl and a brown bag with bread rolls.

Marigold put on her thick new coat, and placed her old one in the fancy box. Someone would surely get use of the coat she'd worn for many years, even if it was old and thin. For the person without a coat of any sort, it would be a Godsend. She knew that from first hand experience.

She juggled the bags as she left the café for the night. "Here, let me," Bunny said, and unlocked the front door. The two women left together, going in different directions. "Goodnight," Bunny said as she turned away.

"Goodnight. I'll see you in the morning. I'll bring back the container then too." Her boss smiled tentatively, and Marigold wondered why. Was it that she'd given Marigold the food? She quickly shook that thought away. It couldn't be that, surely.

She thought back to their earlier conversation, and her mention of her telling Luke the prices were too high. At least that's what she thought Bunny was saying. She tried to shake the thought away. If it was Bunny's business, she would simply reduce the prices if she truly believed the food was overpriced.

Right now she was exhausted beyond belief and couldn't begin to comprehend what it all meant. She continued to walk the few blocks home, and pushed thoughts of Luke to the back of her mind. It didn't last long, and she found herself wondering what Luke was doing right now.

He would be at work, but what sort of work did he do? She knew he didn't work locally, and had to travel two towns over to Grand Falls. It was less than half an hour by buggy, even less by horse, so not that far. Ma had hinted his work was not Godly, but Marigold had no clue what that even meant.

She would have to ask Luke next time she saw him, which would probably be in the morning when they walked to the café together. It was then she realized how snug and warm she was in her new coat. What a wonderful gift Luke had given her, even if she did protest. She did worry about the cost of it though. At a guess, she thought it would be almost a week's wages for her.

She shook herself as she unlocked the front door. If Luke wanted to spoil her, who was she to complain? Her hands full of bags, Ma opened the door before Marigold could do it herself. She stood staring down at her daughter, then reached out and stroked the coat.

"Where did you get that? You know we can't afford it." She continued to stare until Marigold felt uncomfortable.

"It was a gift from Luke," she said, shoving past Ma and into the kitchen. "I have supper. We just have to heat it up."

Ma's frown turned into a grin. Thank goodness she let it slide. An argument was the last thing Marigold wanted now. "Let me," Ma said, taking the bag with the stew. "You've been working hard all day while I've sat about doing nothing."

She smiled tentatively. "I did that for years, so now we're even."

Ma put the stew on to heat up, and poured coffee for them both. "While the food is heating up, I think there are a few things you need to know about Luke Jensen," Ma said after a long silence.

Marigold closed her eyes tightly. She didn't want to know, and what she didn't know wouldn't hurt her right?

"I've told you before, Luke is a bad person," Ma said, reaching over and covering Marigold's hand. "But you have no idea of the extent of it."

Marigold's heart thudded. She wasn't sure she even wanted to know.

Chapter Five

Marigold had spent the night tossing and turning. She'd slept little.

Ma had to be wrong, surely? Luke was not the sort of person Ma made him out to be. He'd help her when she needed it, looked out for her all those years ago, and was still helping her now.

Just because his parents weren't the God-fearing people her mother thought they should be, didn't mean Luke was the same. He went to church with her every week, didn't he? Surely he wouldn't do that if he wasn't a believer?

He even got down on his knees to pray. She'd seen it with her own eyes.

She shuddered. None of it could be true. Not her Luke, the man she'd let kiss her on more than one occasion.

Marigold wondered if he would admit to any of what Ma had said if she asked him.

She sighed. More like *when* she asked him, because she already knew she needed to ask him sooner, rather than later.

Wide awake now, she climbed out of bed and dressed. She filled the stove with wood and set it alight, then filled the kettle. The conversation of last night rolled around in her mind. The way Ma told it, Luke was nothing more than a dirty pimp who forced women to…

No! Luke wasn't like that, she was certain of it. If that were the case, why hadn't he tried to get her to work for him there. He knew she was desperate for money and would have done almost anything.

And that was only half of it. According to Ma he ran a gambling ring. *Stealing food right off the table of desperate families*, she had said. Marigold knew Luke had come from a well-to-do family when they moved into town all those years ago, but she had no idea of their business. If all of what Ma said was true, she would be devastated, and couldn't associate herself with Luke any longer.

If it was true.

She poured herself a strong coffee and slumped down at the table. She was in a state of confusion. The Luke she knew wouldn't involve himself in any of those horrendous activities. *Would he?* Marigold shook herself. *Of course he wouldn't. She had absolutely nothing to worry about.*

Her food felt like nails as it went down her throat, and Marigold found it hard to swallow. What would she say to Luke when he arrived to walk with her this morning? Should she even bring it up?

Of course she would have to ask him at some point. Perhaps this morning was not the right time to do so. She made up her mind not to mention it today. She would ask him after church on Sunday, when they went for their stroll through the park.

Yes, that's what she would do. Sunday wasn't that far away – surely she could wait that long.

It wasn't long until Marigold left for work. She no longer wanted to accept the coat Luke had bought for her, and was in two minds, but decided to wear it. It was far colder inside than normal, so she figured it had to be much colder outside. Besides, he couldn't return it now the coat had been worn.

She shrugged into the plush coat, feeling more than a little guilty. She wasn't sure why she felt so bad – it wasn't her fault Luke had been less than truthful with her, if indeed what Ma said was true. But then again, why would Ma lie about something like that?

At the last moment she remembered the container she needed to return and ran to the kitchen and scooped it up. The memory of last night's stew set her mouth to watering, despite having eaten breakfast not long ago.

She stood at the front door, bracing herself for the cold air that was sure to hit once she opened the door. Instead, Luke Jensen stood outside her door, grinning like a Cheshire cat. She felt like slapping that grin right off his face. But Marigold knew she would never do such a thing. Instead she pursed her lips.

His grin quickly disappeared. "Marigold," he said, moving closer to her. "What's wrong? Has something happened?" He slipped an arm around her shoulder as they began the journey to the café.

She turned her head and stared at him. "Nothing's wrong," she lied, then faced ahead once more. Her whole body stiffened, and it was all she could do not to confront Luke right now.

His hand tightened on her shoulder. "That's not true and we both know it. I've known you far too long to be duped." He suddenly stood in front of her and held both her shoulders. She reluctantly stared into his face and noticed the worry lines, the frown, and the look of disdain on his face.

"I," She'd promised herself not to talk about it now. "I don't want to discuss it now." And she didn't. She wanted to get to work without incidence, without argument, and keep calm so she could enjoy her day at the café. It had become a place of harmony for Marigold despite the busy days, and she wanted to keep it that way.

Without warning, his hands came up and cupped her face. Her heart pounded as he stared into her eyes for what seemed forever, then he slowly bent down and kissed her gently on the lips. He tasted good, and his lips were soft, gentle, as though he really felt something for her. To her dismay, Marigold kissed him back. With passion, no less!

His arms slid up around her back and he pulled her closer to him. She reached around him too. Until she realized what she was doing, then she pushed him away. He stared at her for long moments, then frowned. "Tell me what's wrong." It wasn't a request, it was a demand, and she knew it.

"Not now, and not today."

He stared down at her, as though contemplating her words, then nodded. Finally he came to stand beside her again, and they continued on their way to the café. When they arrived, Luke opened the door for her, as he always did. She paused in the doorway, staring at his handsome face, then glanced at the ground. "I don't think you should come in today, Luke," she said, then turned to go inside.

He grabbed her gently by the wrist, his jaw working furiously. "Tell me what's wrong," he ground out under his breath. Then suddenly his eyes opened wide, and he went white. He mumbled under his breath and Marigold couldn't make out the words, although she though he said something about 'interfering'. However, she couldn't be certain.

He grabbed her by the arm and marched her to a table in the far corner. "Sit!" he demanded, then hurried into the kitchen where Bunny could be found. He quickly returned with two coffees. He placed one in front of her, and the other he continued to hold, then took a long mouthful.

He stared at her over his coffee.

"I know what this is about," he said barely holding his temper in check. He'd always had a temper, and mother had regularly told him to count to ten. Right now he was convinced fifty was probably more appropriate.

She stared at him, her pretty face marred with a mixture of anger and disappointment. What had Maggie Davis said to her? Oh, he was certain that miserable woman had gotten to Marigold; she'd had it in for him since her husband began visiting his parent's establishment all those years ago. The last thing he wanted to do was tarnish the memory of her father, but how did he keep the man's memory intact while asserting his own sense of worth? It was not going to be an easy task.

"Ma told me…" she said with no prompting. He'd know all along it was that wretched woman. She had always blamed his parents for her husband's wrong-doing, his addiction. When they were dead and buried, she'd blamed Luke. Her wrath was misplaced, and he was certain deep down she must know it.

He reached over and captured her hand in his. "Your Ma has prejudices that are ill-founded."

She took another sip of coffee and stared at him over the rim of her cup. "Do you own a…" She swallowed hard as though she dare not say the word.

"I own a saloon, yes."

She closed her eyes tightly, as though fighting back tears. But none surfaced. "Ma says you own a…brothel." She said the last word quickly, as though saying it faster might make it a lie.

"I inherited my parent's business, that is true." He squeezed her hand tightly, as the first customer of the day came into the café.

"I have to get to work," she said, fidgeting about on her chair.

He held her hand in an effort to keep her there. "Stay," he demanded. She stared at him, anger written across her face. "Please. I've cleared it with Bunny." Marigold leaned back and sighed. She was clearly unhappy with the situation, but he needed for her to understand. "My father wasn't..." He paused. Saying the words out loud made it true. "He wasn't a particularly nice person," he said quietly.

The color drained from her face. "So it's true. You're a pimp." Tears welled in her eyes as she said the dreaded word.

He took a deep breath before answering. "It's not like that," he said. Before he could explain further, she fled to the kitchen. Where Bunny was. If she asked, he was certain Bunny would give up the whole story despite him asking her not to. She'd said all along if Marigold asked, she wouldn't lie to her, and he didn't blame her.

He took another mouthful of coffee and slumped over the table. He couldn't bare to lose Marigold. She was the love of his life, and had been since the day they'd met. The last thing he wanted was for her to have half-truths about his business. He also didn't want to tell her about her depraved father. That was her mother's job.

He glanced up when she stood in front of him, a plate of hot food in her hands. The fact she even stood there gave him some hope, although if he was honest with himself, Marigold would feel obligated. She was being paid to do a job, and she would fulfill her obligations no matter what.

"Thank you," he said quietly as she placed the food in front of him. Her face remained expressionless.

His heart shattered.

It had taken all her effort to smile at the customers.

Luke was long gone, and she'd felt both relieved and disappointed. They hadn't resolved anything, and it left her feeling drained. Was Ma telling the truth, or as Luke suggested, did she only give Marigold part of the story?

They'd known each other for such a long time, and never had she known Luke to be an unlawful person. He may have skirted the law at times, but she'd never know him to actually break the law. He'd never once harmed her, and to her knowledge, he'd never harmed anyone else.

She had to admit though, he had been very secretive about his work. That had never sat well with Marigold, and now she knew why. She swallowed hard. Right now she was working, and she had to keep her composure for the sake of the customers. Besides, Bunny was counting on her.

Taking her bucket of soapy water and a cloth, she went to the back of the café and began to clean down the tables ready for the noon rush. She piled soiled dishes on a tray, then cleaned down the tables, ensuring the chairs were clean, and the condiments were filled.

Along with the soiled dishes, there were abandoned newspapers. Customers brought their newspaper with them, reading while they ate. A terrible habit as far as Marigold was concerned, but they did it regularly. She really wished they would take them back with them. They made a dreadful mess of the tables, not to mention her hands.

As she went to close this particular one, her eyes fell to a column headed *Love Struck* – it piqued her interest. As she scanned the column, Marigold discovered it was a column where desperate people could write for advice about their love life. Was *she* desperate enough to write to *Love Struck?*

She quickly scanned the remainder of the short column. Most of the responses were quite good, and seemed appropriate, helpful even. Her mind made up, Marigold ripped the column out of the newspaper and shoved it into her pocket. Tonight she would write, and hopefully get advise on what to do about Luke.

Trouble was, she'd already fallen hard for him, even if he only saw her as a distraction. Soon he would move on to someone less judgmental, she was certain.

Chapter Six

They had leftovers from the café again for supper –
this time it was roast lamb and roasted vegetables.
An absolute luxury for her and Ma. After they'd
eaten, Ma helped her with the dishes, then Marigold
sat down and re-read the newspaper article – more
than once. None of the senders used their real
names, and neither would she. Besides, she didn't
want the world to know she needed advice about her
love life.

Rehearsing her own letter in her head, she finally sat at the writing desk and penned a letter.

Dear Love Struck,

I am beside myself with worry. This next birthday, just months away, I will turn twenty-six at which time I will officially be an old maid. I'm of medium height with long golden hair, and have been told I'm rather too thin. I'd probably fatten up somewhat with love and care.

The only eligible men around here are bad boy types, and although they do appeal in some ways, I'm not sure I want to go down that road.

I'm doomed to loneliness for the rest of my life unless I find a suitable man to marry.

Can you help?

Sincerely,

Miserable in Montana

Marigold read it quietly so Ma couldn't hear, then ripped the letter up. She wasn't being at all truthful, so started over.

Dear Love Struck,

I have fallen in love with a man who I'm told is not a good person. Ma says he's a bad boy and I should keep my distance. She's told me some terrible things about his father, and I'm afraid he may be following in his father's footsteps.

He hasn't said he loves me, but he treats me special, even helped me get a decent job. I don't want to give him up, even after what my Ma told me.

What should I do?

Sincerely,

Miserable in Montana

"What's this then?" Ma's voice caused her to jump, and Marigold covered the letter with her hands.

She stared up at her mother feeling rather resentful. Perhaps she shouldn't, but she was blissfully happy, and unaware of Luke's saloon business before Ma opened her mouth. "It's private," she said, then scooped up the letter and shoved it in an envelope. She wondered how long it would take to get an answer.

Even more important, how long before she forgave Ma for shattering her previously happy world with Luke?

She wasn't certain either of those would happen, but it was certainly worth the risk of posting the letter. She would do that on the way to work in the morning. More likely than not, Luke wouldn't turn up in the morning anyway. She would leave a few minutes early to compensate for her short deviation.

"What do you mean private?" Ma sounded annoyed. Marigold had never kept secrets from her before. They'd always been open with each other in the past, but now she wasn't so sure. She had the distinct feeling Ma hadn't told her the whole story. Something didn't seem quite right. Rather than push for an answer, Marigold would try to go about her business as though nothing had happened.

Only she knew that was not possible. Her world had shattered last night when she found out Luke owned a saloon, not to mention the brothel he ran on the premises. Everything Luke did for a living went against her Christian upbringing. She was surprised, and even annoyed he had attended church with her. How did he sit in church, on his knees praying no less, when he knew what he did for a living went against the teachings of the bible?

Marigold forced back a sob. The last thing she wanted was to cry in front of Ma. After all, she should feel nothing but hatred for Luke Jensen right now. Instead she felt disappointment, but even more, she still felt deeply for the man she thought she knew. And it tore her heart into tiny pieces.

With a heavy heart, she headed for bed. Whether she would sleep or not, remained to be seen. No matter what happened, she had to work tomorrow. Finally she'd found a steady job with good money. Ma now had the life she deserved.

Marigold changed into her nightgown and climbed into bed. Luke drifted through her mind as she fell into a light slumber.

Luke waited outside Marigold's front door for what seemed like forever. But she never appeared. He was on time, so he figured he couldn't have missed her. It was unlike her not to go to work, and he had no intention of knocking. What if Maggie Davis answered? He wasn't sure he'd be able to contain his temper. Instead he wandered down to the café.

And there she was – Marigold was in the coffee nook preparing for the morning rush. Did she purposely leave home early to avoid him? His heart thudded. Was it over between them? He hoped not, he was far too much in love with her to lose her.

Blast her interfering mother. He'd had every intention of telling Marigold about his job – the saloon and the brothel, but in his own time. He wanted to wait until she was in love with him, and didn't want to give him up. Selfish? For sure, but he loved her beyond anything he'd ever imagined possible.

Kissing her behind the church all those years ago, who would have believed her to be his soulmate? He wasn't often honest with himself, especially when it came to women, but Luke now knew he couldn't live without his sweet and innocent Marigold. She was the most beautiful woman he'd ever met, and had a heart of gold.

He intended to win back that heart and never let her go. His heart thudded again. What would he do if he couldn't win her back?

He stood at the entrance to the café watching her work. He wanted to go to her and wrap his arms around her, but Luke knew she would shrug him away. Not only because she was working, but because she was angry at him. As he opened the door wider, her head shot up. It was as if she sensed him there. It gave him a glimmer of hope.

"Marigold," he said breathlessly. He watched as she pulled her bottom lip in. It was a nervous reaction she sometimes had. He'd noticed it before, usually when she was undecisive about something. He took a few steps toward her, and she stepped back. Resigned to not holding her after all, he stared at her momentarily, then headed toward a small table at the back. He sat there most days, away from the crowd, where he could have a bit of peace and quiet.

He'd not long removed his coat and sat down when she approached him, and his heartbeat quickened. "Coffee?" She knew he would and didn't wait for an answer.

He nodded anyway. "I missed you this morning," he said softly.

It was her turn to nod. "I had to post a letter so left early."

He stared into her face. Her beautiful yet saddened face. "What was so important?" She turned her face away from him. What was she hiding?

He took a mouthful of coffee and watched her. She warred with herself trying to decide whether or not to tell him, Luke was certain. "It's personal." The moment the words were out, she turned and walked away, moving to another table and another customer. He knew he shouldn't, but Luke felt a burning jealousy for the recipient of that coffee. He wanted her here with him, talking to him, spending her time with him, and not some stranger.

He began to count under his breath. He'd not felt this way before, so it made sense this was brought about because of what Maggie Davis had told her daughter. Luke wasn't certain yet what that was, but he knew it wasn't good. At least not good for him. More than likely the woman had added her own version of events, and not the way they'd actually happened.

By the time Marigold served his breakfast he was fuming. Not at her, his anger would never be focused on her. He was holding his temper in check, but only just. He reached out and grabbed her hand as she walked away. She said not a word, but turned to stare at him.

"Is there a problem with the food," she asked as though nothing was wrong. He stared up at her, then kissed the back of her hand.

He shook his head. Words didn't come, and it was as though there was a huge lump in his throat. Luke continued to stare, then stood. He scooped her around the waist with his hands, and held her close. "I missed you this morning," he whispered, ensuring no one else heard the conversation.

She rested her head on his shoulder, and Luke felt a modicum of relief. The fact she'd done that assured him they were not finished. That they still had a chance.

Her arms slipped up around him, and he felt more certain than he was a few minutes ago. She still felt something for him. His heart pounded. He lifted her chin with his fingers, and faced her toward him, ready to take her lips. She stared up into his face.

She was the most beautiful creature he'd ever laid eyes on. What was he going to do if he lost her? He felt hollow – similar to when his parents had been killed. He made up his mind then and there that he couldn't lose her, and he had to do whatever it took to make sure it didn't happen.

He searched her face, and watched as she licked her lips. It was far too much temptation, and he swooped down and kissed her. Luke didn't care how many customers were in café. Marigold was his girl, and he would kiss her if that's what he wanted.

She suddenly stepped back. "Luke," she said softly. "I have work to do."

Disappointment filled him. Would he ever get to kiss her again? Or even hold her? His heart shattered all over again, but he let her go. He watched as she went from table to table looking after the customers. They all loved her, it was plain to see.

But no one loved her as much as he did. And no one ever would.

Each day they went through the motions. Luke collected her from home in the morning, he walked her to work, had breakfast then left.

Somehow he had got to a point of holding her hand for the duration of their walk to the café. As they arrived, she pulled out of his grip, and despite her obvious denial, he'd seen the look of disappointment on her face once they were apart.

Things were different between them, and it broke his heart. They were meant to be together, he knew they were. The first time he'd held her at the church dance all those years ago he'd known it. She'd been more than a little reserved with her parents watching them, but he felt it. She had fallen under his spell. He felt it in his heart.

It was the reason he'd dragged her out behind the church hall. He wanted to make her his own by kissing her. At first it was like a game, but when they got to their destination, she stared at him so intensely, it was all he could do to resist. He backed her up against the wall, out of sight, with no chance of being seen. Then he'd placed himself in front of her, blocking her in, his arms either side of her. At first Marigold had looked terrified, but he'd reassured her he wouldn't harm her, and she'd relaxed a little.

"I'm going to kiss you," he'd whispered, and then he did. At first she resisted, but then relaxed. He pulled her closer, and like any teenage boy, had reveled in the feel of her maturing body close to his. Suddenly she'd pulled away and stared up at him, her fingers to her lips. Then she ran.

Until recently, he'd never managed to kiss her again despite their many brief encounters over the years.

The thought of that day had seen him through all these difficult years without her. As much as he'd been given the tag of bad boy, he had saved himself for Marigold. If he lost her now, he'd be devasted. Life wasn't worth living with out her.

His head shot up as he realized she was standing in front of him. "I said, do you want more coffee?" She stood there looking down at him, her eyes filled with sadness. He suddenly kicked back his chair and reached for her, almost causing her to drop the pot of coffee.

"What I want," he said, taking the pot from her, "Is to hold you, and to kiss you."

He watched as heat crept up her neck and then her face. He pulled her tightly to him, and just held her for long moments. He studied her, trying to decide if she was compliant or would deny him, then leaned down and kissed her, letting everyone in the room know that Marigold Davis was his girl, and he intended for her to be his wife.

Her hand reached up and touched his cheek, then she rested her head against his shoulder. "I've really missed you, Luke," she said quietly, and he pulled her closer still.

Chapter Seven

Finally, after all this time, the letter she'd been waiting for had arrived. Her letter from *Love Struck*.

Each day, when she'd managed to elicit a short break, she ran all the way to the post office to check if her letter had arrived. She'd done that now for nearly three weeks, and finally it arrived. She shoved the unopened letter into her skirt pocket and ran back to the café. Bunny had allowed her this one luxury each day.

Marigold had admitted to Bunny about the letter, and about her indecision about Luke. She'd opened her mouth to say something, then changed her mind. There was some dark secret that Bunny was withholding, she was certain of it. When she'd confessed what Ma had said about Luke, she was certain Bunny had something to tell her, but she kept her secret close to her heart.

Although it annoyed Marigold, a promise is a promise, and if her boss had promised to keep someone's secret, even if it affected Marigold, then she couldn't complain. What if she'd shared a secret with Bunny and she told? She'd be more than a little angry about it. No, she couldn't blame the woman for withholding vital information. Even if it did make her decision more difficult.

She arrived back at the café not long before the noon rush, her heart pounding. "Well, did it arrive?" Bunny asked, as she had done every day.

She reached into her skirt pocket and pulled out the neatly addressed envelope. "It did!" Marigold said excitedly. "I haven't opened it yet."

"Then open it!!"

Marigold turned the envelope over and began to rip open the sealed envelope. Her head shot up as the door to the café opened. Their first luncheon customer, and he wouldn't be the last. With a heavy heart, she shoved the letter back into her skirt pocket.

"Later," Bunny whispered. "It won't change anything now." She returned to the kitchen, and Marigold saw to their customers.

It wasn't long before Luke arrived, and her heart fluttered. No matter what Ma said, being in the same room as Luke did things to her. How could loving someone this much feel so wrong? She felt him staring at her and lifted her head. Their eyes met, and the two stood staring at each other for far too long. Marigold had work to do, and Luke was a distraction she didn't need right now.

She scooped up a mug and along with the coffee pot, headed to his table. After she'd poured his coffee, he reached out and held her hand. The want in his eyes was almost overwhelming. "Sit down and talk to me," he said quietly. "I've missed you far too much today."

She threw him the hint of a smile. How she would love to do that, but the customers were piling in now, and she had to tend to them. "You know I can't. Look around – the café is filling up already."

He glanced about. "I don't really care," he whispered. "Let them wait."

She was shocked at his words, and didn't know how to reply, so she didn't. Instead she wrenched her hand out of his, and walked away.

"Marigold…" she heard him call after her. It took all her effort to ignore him. She scurried into the kitchen and picked up the first order, then delivered it. She glanced across at Luke who gazed at her with longing. How she would love to go to him.

No matter what Ma said, she still loved Luke. Loved him far too much for her liking. It was clouding her judgement. Perhaps *Love Struck* would put things into perspective for her. Marigold reached down into her pocket and fingered the envelope. She longed to open it right now and read the words. Hopefully words of reassurance, but she had to prepare herself for the worst scenario.

Bunny dinged the bell, indicating the next meal was ready to be served. She almost ran in the kitchen, happy to be away from Luke's constant scrutiny. Today he'd ordered Chicken Pot Pie, and now she had to deliver it to him. She glanced up at Bunny. "Can't you serve him?"

The cook's head shot up. "I'm sorry. I would if I had time, but I simply don't." She looked remorseful, and Marigold suddenly felt bad for even suggesting it.

"No, I'm sorry," she said quietly. "I shouldn't have asked." She carried the meal out to Luke's table, and watched as a grin spread across his face. No matter the circumstances, he was always pleased to see her.

Walking toward his table felt like it took hours, but it was only twenty seconds at most. He watched her every move, which made her feel self-conscious. It shouldn't, this very same thing happened every day he came here to eat.

She placed the meal in front of him, and as he'd done every time she approached his table he snatched up her hand. Today though he kissed the back of her palm. A shudder went through her.

"I thought we could go for a drive Sunday after church," he said quietly. "I can hire a carriage, and we can go into the hills." He eyes begged her to say yes.

"I," *Should she go?* Much as she wanted, they would be unchaperoned. She stared down into his handsome face. He looked tired, ragged even, and she wondered if she was the cause of that.

"Don't say no. *Please?*" He almost begged her and she felt suddenly guilty. Should she reply before reading *Love Struck's* letter? Should she even place her future on a letter? Her heart pounded thinking about it all.

Her train of thought was interrupted by the bell in the kitchen. "I have to go," she said, then scurried off.

She glanced back over her shoulder momentarily, and saw Luke had begun eating. Was she merely a distraction while he waited for his food? Sometimes she thought so. Other times she thought it was simply Luke taking care of himself. Once he was at work, he didn't eat for hours. She couldn't deny him the self-care he needed to practice.

"Hearty beef and vegetable soup with hot rolls," Bunny said. "Mr Jenkins." Marigold nodded absently, then delivered the meal to the customer. She noticed his coffee was empty, and scurred back for the coffee pot, filling his mug. She glanced up and saw Luke indicate his mug needed filling too. Only when she arrived, it was totally full.

"Sorry," he said. "I just wanted you near me." He grinned at her, and she scowled. His grin soon disappeared.

"I'm busy," she snapped at him, then hurried back to the coffee hub. For a moment she forgot he was a paying customer too. She shouldn't have gone off at him like that, but he tried her patience some days. She stared his way, only to find him staring back, pain written all over his face.

She refilled the pot then headed to his table. At the very least she would clear away his soiled dishes. "I apologize," she said as she piled the dishes onto a tray. "I shouldn't have reacted that way."

His arm snaked up around her waist, and her heart pounded. His touch always sent fire blazing through her. As much as she fought it, just being near him did things to her. "Yes," she said, then stared down at him. "I'll come with you Sunday."

He stood and pulled her closer. "If there was space, I'd pick you up and twirl you about." He would too. He'd done it before, on more than one occasion.

"Then I am more than a little pleased there is no space," she said seriously, then grinned at him, and waited for his kiss. She licked her lips in anticipation.

Luke stood staring, hovering over her. The longer he studied her, the more she wanted him to kiss her. Did he do that on purpose? Was he trying to torment her, to make her want him more? She suspected the answer was yes to all those questions. "Well, I have to get back to work now," she said, staring into his eyes.

"You are nothing but a minx," he whispered, then leaned down and kissed her. Marigold leaned into him. She loved the feel of him, reveled in being in his arms, and enjoyed it very much when he kissed her.

How could she even contemplate giving up this man? She needed to read the letter and make her decision before it was too late to turn back.

A thought struck her. Perhaps it was far too late already.

The rest of the day went slowly. Customers trickled in over the next few hours, some wanted coffee only, others wanted cake as well.

Then the rush for supper began. Marigold was anxious to open and read her letter, but simply didn't have the time. As things slowed down in the café, she began to scrub down the tables ready for the next day, when they would do it all over again.

"Come on then," Bunny insisted, when the last customer left and she locked the door behind him. "What does it say?"

Marigold snatched the letter out of her skirt pocket. She held it out in front of her, then pulled it close and breathed in. There was the slightest aroma of perfume. As she'd already guessed, *Love Struck* was a woman.

She tore at the envelope and pulled the letter out. For just a moment Marigold stared at the folded paper, her heart pounding. Did this letter hold the key to her happiness?

"Oh for goodness sakes," Bunny snapped, then reach over and tried to grab it, almost ripping the delicate paper. Marigold was surprised – in her wildest dreams she didn't suspect Bunny would do such a thing. "I'm sorry. I shouldn't have done that," Bunny said, in her most apologetic voice.

"It's fine." Marigold unfolded the paper slowly, being far more careful since the paper was torn.

Dear Miserable in Montana,

It sounds to me as though you are completely in love with your young man. Most likely it's too late for you to have second thoughts – if you're as much in love as you say.

While your mother may have an unpopular opinion of your true love, you are the one who will spend the rest of your life with him should he propose. If you can't bring her around to your way of thinking, you may, after all have to give him up.

Are you certain you're not interested in bad boys? They might not be so bad after all. (And this one sounds quite appealing.)

Yours Truly,

Love Struck

Marigold read the letter, then read it again. "I waited all this time for nothing," she said, quite annoyed.

She then handed the letter to Bunny who read it carefully.

"What do you think it says?" Bunny studied her, and she wasn't quite sure what to make of it.

She snatched the letter back and began to fold it, ready to stuff into the envelope. "That I have to give Luke up because Ma hates him."

"Let me see that again." Bunny stared at her, then re-read the letter. "That is not how I read it. But it's your letter, not mine," she said handing the letter back. She then began to fill a container with cornbread, biscuits and stew. There was even some leftover blackberry cobbler.

Marigold studied the letter again. "Are you sure?"

"Sure as I can be," Bunny said, then handed her the bag full of food. "Time to go before the sky becomes dark. I'll see you tomorrow."

"Thank you," Marigold said, then hugged Bunny as best she could with her hands full. They'd become very close over the past few weeks, and to be honest, she wasn't sure what she would do without the woman who was not only her boss, but had become her friend and confidante.

She strolled home in the semi-darkness, contemplating the letter. She needed to read it again, but that couldn't happen with Ma around. And what did *Love Struck* mean about getting Ma on side? She wasn't sure that could ever happen. Ma hated Luke with all her heart. Marigold was far from certain that would ever change.

Entering the kitchen, she prepared their supper, not saying much at all. It was a problem that would take a lot of solving, and she wasn't sure it was even possible.

"Supper smells delicious," Ma said, bringing Marigold out of her thoughts. She put on a brave face. Ma had no idea how much her heart had shattered.

Chapter Eight

Marigold strolled to the livery, her arm through Luke's. They'd packed a picnic lunch and headed out straight after church.

Ma was not happy about her going unchaperoned, but Marigold was almost beyond caring what Ma thought. She was constantly coming between her and Luke, and that just wouldn't do.

After reading and re-reading her letter from *Love Struck*, Marigold made the decision to continue seeing Luke. Whether or not that came to anything, she had no idea. She loved Luke, but he didn't love her. Nonetheless, she enjoyed his company.

He helped her climb up onto the carriage, and his touch sent a thrill through her, as it always did. Once she was settled, he climbed up himself, pulling a thick woolen blanket around their knees. The days continued to be chilly, and Marigold wore her luxurious coat gifted to her by Luke, which kept out most of the cold. She didn't really need the blanket, but said not a word. She enjoyed being close to Luke, and hoped he liked being close to her too.

"Shall we go?" he asked, not waiting for an answer, then snapped the reins for the horses to move, and covered her hand with his own.

It didn't take long for them to arrive at the foot of the mountain, twenty minutes perhaps, but Luke ventured further in until they were deep into the forest. Marigold felt somewhat afraid. She wasn't frightened of Luke, she would never feel that way, but she was afraid they may get lost.

She tightened her grip on his hand. He turned to face her. "Is everything alright?"

"Do you know the way," she whispered, having no idea why she whispered as they were the only people around. "I'm afraid we may get lost."

He grinned at her then quickened the pace of the horses. "Not a chance. There's a small clearing over there by the river. I thought we could picnic there." He studied her, apparently waiting for some sort of reaction, so she nodded.

"Oooh, it's lovely," she said as they pulled into the clearing. Luke climbed down, tying the horses to a nearby bush, then helped her down. He grabbed her around the waist, and held her halfway, staring into her face as he did so. "Are you going to put me down?" she asked when he seemed to have no inclination to place her on solid ground.

He slowly brought her down and steadied her, but he didn't let go. His hands were firmly planted around her waist. "You are incredibly beautiful," he said quietly, then held her close. She rested her head against his shoulder, not sure how to answer, or even if she should.

Suddenly her head snapped up. She shouldn't be doing this. Not here, not alone and without a chaperone. As much as she hated to admit it, Ma was right; this was a very bad idea. She pulled away and began to wander over to the river's edge. She leaned down and let the water roll over her fingers. "The water is freezing!" she said as she straightened up, and Luke came to her side.

"Let me warm you up," he said, taking her hands in his own. He lifted her hand and kissed the back of it, then enveloped her hand, warming it as he'd promised. "I love coming to this place," he told her.

"It was the one thing we did as a family. Once a month after church we'd come here. We didn't move to the area until I was a teenager, as you know, but I adored coming here. Father and I would fish, and Mother would simply sit and relax. The rest of the week we worked."

Marigold could see they were fond memories for him. "I can see why you liked it here. It's wonderful," she said. "So peaceful."

He turned to her. It was then she saw the sadness in his eyes. "That wasn't it at all. It was the one time my parents didn't act like money-hungry monsters. They were simply Mother and Father."

For the first time, Marigold was beginning to understand Luke. She'd had no idea his childhood had been so difficult. She'd erroneously assumed because he'd lived a privileged life, it was all honey and roses. She couldn't have been further from the truth.

He shook his head. "Forget all that. Today is about us. About making new memories with just the two of us."

She liked that thought. Memories of her and Luke – that sounded wonderful. But how long would they last? If she had her way, it would be forever, but what about Ma? She threatened to stand between them, and as much as Marigold didn't want her to do that, she also didn't want to lose Luke.

Her dilemma was suffocating her.

He studied her as he continued to warm her hand. "What are you thinking?" He looked at her curiously, as though he was trying to read her mind.

She shook her head. "Oh, it's nothing really." She stepped away from him and glanced about. "It really is lovely here. Perhaps we could go for a short stroll?" He offered her his arm, and they moved out of the clearing into the density of the trees. She shuddered. Marigold wasn't sure if it was because of the coldness compared to the clearing, or whether it was because she was alone with Luke in an unfamiliar place.

"Cold?" His arm was suddenly around her waist, and warmth filled her.

She turned to face him. "Not really. I, I don't really know what I feel. Foreboding perhaps." She tried to smile, but right now that would be a lie. "Can we go back, Luke? I don't feel comfortable here."

"Of course." He didn't seem angry or upset, and totally accepted her discomfort.

"There's something I want to talk to you about," he said gently as they returned to the horses. Was he breaking up with her? If their roles were reversed, Marigold would certainly consider it. Ma was a formidable opponent, and not one to back down without a fight. She would wear anyone down.

"It's Ma, isn't it?" she said without thinking. "She's only trying to protect me."

He stopped walking and studied her again. "Your Ma can be pretty scary, but no, that's not what I wanted to talk to you about." He put his hands to her shoulders, and stared at her lips. She waited for his kiss, and almost sank into him. Luke cupped her face, and as if deciding on his next move, simply stood there as though checking her out. Finally he leaned in and kissed her.

She sighed at the feel of his lips. She'd always thought they were meant to be together, and now she was convinced of it. Marigold wanted nothing more than to be with Luke. Only one thing got in the way of that, and it was Ma.

When he ended the kiss, Luke held her at arms length and stared at her. He said not a word for a full minute, a frown on his face.

"Is something wrong?" Her heart thudded. Now she was certain he was breaking up with her. She squeezed her eyes tight together. "You're breaking up with me," she said, her voice full of emotion.

As she tried to turn away from him, Luke pulled her back to face him. "You couldn't be further from the truth," he said quietly. "I love you, Marigold, more than you will ever know." He pulled her to him and held her tight.

Her heart pounded in her chest. Luke loved her? He truly loved her? This was the best news, and was totally unexpected. "I love you too," she said softly. "I didn't know you loved me." Tears trickled from her eyes, and she swiped at them. But they had a problem and they both knew it.

He stared at her with sadness. "This is meant to be a happy time," he said, then suddenly dropped to one knee. "Marigold," he said, reaching for her hand. "Will you marry me?"

She stared down at him in disbelief. He was asking the impossible. How could they marry when her mother hated him? On the other hand Marigold loved him. They were soulmates and meant to be together.

She swallowed hard. "I, I want to," she said softly, not saying no, but not saying yes either.

He stood to face her. "We have a problem though," he said, his frown returning.

Marigold stared up into his handsome face. "Ma." No other words were necessary. They both knew Maggie Davis would come between them if they let her.

"We'll sort it out," Luke said. "I promise." Marigold had no idea how he would convince her mother, but if anyone could do it, Luke could.

~*~

Luke knocked on the front door to Marigold's home, his heart pounding. This would be amongst the hardest things he'd ever had to do.

The door flew open and the vindictive woman stared at him. "What are you doin' here?" Maggie Davis snapped. "Marigold's at work." She began to push the door closed in his face.

Luke quickly shoved his foot in the way to stop her closing it. "I know Marigold is at work. I escorted her there as I do every morning." He smiled at her, but she didn't return his gesture. Instead she appeared even more irritated. "I came to see you," he said, trying to keep the annoyance out of his voice. "May I come in?"

"Hurumph!" She flung the door open and headed toward what Luke recalled was the sitting room. He stood in the doorway to that room, not prepared to anger the woman further by assuming anything. "Well, go on, sit down," she snapped. "You'll make me neck ache if I have to stare up at ya."

He wanted to grin, but thought the better of it and forced himself into no expression at all. "Mrs Davis," he said once he was seated. "I want to discuss your daughter."

She turned to him and stared with angry eyes. Then she suddenly stood. "I'm gettin' a coffee. You want one?" It was blatantly obvious she didn't want to talk to him, and only offered him coffee out of convention.

"Thank you, yes," he said, also standing. If that's what it took to get her to discuss Marigold with him, he was willing to comply.

He stood in the doorway between the kitchen and sitting room and watched her pull down two mugs. The kettle was already boiling on the stove. He'd no doubt interrupted her morning coffee when he'd arrived.

"I usually have me coffee out 'ere in the kitchen." She indicated the kitchen table, and he sat, not willing to cause an upset that would stop the discussion. She made the coffee and banged it on the table in front of him, causing it to slosh over the sides.

"Right. What is it you wanna say? Get it over with." She lifted her mug slowly, watching his every move over the top of the rim as it reached her mouth.

"It's about Marigold," he said gently.

She pursed her lips, as he knew she would. The woman hated him with a vengeance, through no fault of his own. "What about 'er?"

He swallowed. She wasn't making it easy for him, but of course she wouldn't. Maggie Davis hated him. Hated what he stood for, too.

"Marigold and I, we've been stepping out these past months."

"Hurumph." This time she adjusted her shoulders. *Anything to annoy him*, Luke thought.

He took a deep breath. This wasn't going well, not that he expected anything else. "I'm just going to say it, Mrs Davis. I intend to marry your daughter." He said the last words faster than he'd anticipated, but now they were said, and he could breathe again.

"Over my dead body," Mrs Davis bellowed, then lifted her coffee again as though nothing had happened.

He quirked an eyebrow at her. "You do realize your daughter is almost twenty-six? That she can make her own decisions without your permission?"

The woman stared at him. He suddenly understood that old saying; *if looks could kill*.

"I know you blame me for what happened to your husband, Claude. Marigold's father." He let his words sink in for a moment or two. "I was a mere teenager at the time. It wasn't my fault…"

"Then whose fault was it?" she snapped.

He put down his mug and studied her. He said his carefully chosen words slowly. "Your husband made the decision to frequent my parent's saloon." He watched as she sat rigid, then swallowed. "He also made the decision to take advantage of the soiled doves there. No one forced him." He stopped momentarily and assessed her reaction, then continued when she said nothing. "My father was not a good person," he said honestly. "But he didn't force Claude into anything he didn't want to do."

She went white and drifted sideways. Luke thought she might faint and began to stand. She waved him back onto his seat. "I'm alright," she said quietly. She took another sip of her coffee, then straightened her shoulders. "My Claude, 'e wasn't a good man." She stared down into her coffee mug. "He wasn't a good 'usband, and he was an even worse father." She glanced up at him, her eyes brimming with tears. "He died because he cheated at cards, I know that, but 'ow do I tell Marigold?"

Right then Luke didn't know what to say. He was never speechless, but right this moment he was. Maggie Davis had just admitted Claude's death wasn't anyone's fault but his own.

"It wasn't your fault. It wasn't even your father's fault, the mongrel that 'e was." She closed her eyes briefly, then opened them again. "I needed someone to blame, and since he's no longer 'ere, I blamed you. I, I'm truly sorry, Luke." She took a long sip of coffee, then spoke again. "My Marigold, she loves you, and more than anything, I want 'er to be happy."

Luke stared. Did Mrs Davis just apologize to him? After all these years the woman admitted she was wrong? His heart pounded. Perhaps things would work out after all.

It was a like a fairytale, and Marigold still didn't believe this was her reality.

Luke had arranged for her wedding gown to be made by Clara Petersen, the owner of the *Honey Blossom Boutique*. She'd insisted she didn't need a wedding gown, but Luke would have none of it.

So there she stood now, at the entrance of the tiny church in Harrietville, where she'd attended every Sunday for most of her life. Clara fussed over her gown, ensuring it was perfect. Ma stood proudly beside her, waiting to walk her down the aisle to her one true love.

"You look wonderful, Ma," she said. "Luke has been so generous to both of us."

Ma nodded. "That he has. I'll never be able to thank him enough."

"He doesn't want thanks, Ma. He just wants us in his life." Her head shot up as the organ music began to play. "Well, I guess it's time."

The entrance door was opened, and they stepped inside. Marigold clutched her bouquet of fresh flowers that Luke had arranged for her. She reached up and touched the hat that sat on the side of her head. Clara had outdone herself with both the gown and hat.

If someone had told Marigold a year ago she would be wearing *Honey Blossom Boutique* clothing, she would have laughed in their face. She still found it hard to believe.

After the wedding today, Luke had promised he would move Ma into his big house as well. It brought a tear to her eye that Ma would finally get the life she deserved.

As they arrived down the front of the small chapel, Luke turned to face her. His hand came up and he gently brushed her cheek. "I love you," he said quietly. Ma handed Marigold over to her groom.

"Dearly Beloved," the preacher began. Marigold hung on his every word. "You may now kiss your bride," he finished, and Luke did exactly that.

He offered her his arm and they left the church. She still couldn't believe she'd married her teenage sweetheart. Luke Jensen was her first crush, and no one else had ever lived up to him. She was ecstatic he'd waited for her. Not that she'd truly expected to marry him – it was a teenage dream, and not something she expected to come true.

As they stood in the entrance to the chapel, rice was thrown their way. Marigold glanced about at their guests. Bunny was near the front, and tears trickled down her face.

Bunny! Dear Bunny. What would she do now? Luke had made it clear she no longer needed to work. "I have it covered," he said. "I've already found a replacement. Besides," he'd said. "You'll be busy with our babies." He grinned at her, and Marigold knew she'd gone beet red.

Epilogue

Three and a half years later...

"No, Tommy. Don't do that," Marigold said, exasperation in her voice. Baby Thomas was just beginning to crawl. Everything was fair game, and he was having fun exploring.

"He's just a baby," Ma said, snatching up her ten-month-old grandson. "You wait until he's a bit older and into everything."

Marigold sighed. "I thought he already was into everything." She leaned back in her chair. "Thanks Ma. I don't know what I would do without you."

Ma patted Tommy's back until the child was lulled into sleep. "I'm sure you'd managed," she said quietly. "But I do love living here, and getting to know my grandchildren so much better than if we lived apart."

"Luke wouldn't have it any other way, and neither would I." She was suddenly on her feet. "Elizabeth! Leave that Christmas tree alone!" Marigold sighed, then rubbed her very swollen belly. "By the time Tommy is Elizabeth's age, this one will be nearly ready to crawl." She sighed again as Luke entered the room, then sat down, unable to stand any longer.

Luke came and sat beside her. "I did warn you I wanted lots of babies," he said, a grin on his face. "We have a big house with far too many bedrooms."

Luke was a good father – the best. Claude was not a good father, Marigold had decided long ago. Even before Ma had explained what happened, that he'd been shot by another gambler when he'd cheated, she'd known he wasn't a good father. Or even a good man.

It had haunted her for years, but finally knowing the truth had helped to chase the ghosts away.

On the other hand, Luke was amongst the best of them. It wasn't the big house, or the expensive clothes. It wasn't even the maid he insisted they have. It was the fact he spent time with his family. He'd told her much about his terrible upbringing since they married, and had long decided his children would not endure the same.

His business was thriving, even more than it had been before, but since Luke had installed a manager, he'd been able to cut back his hours. He wanted to spend more time with his family, and Marigold admired him for it.

She was far from pleased when she discovered he owned a saloon, and she was terribly upset about the brothel. He'd explained he didn't own the brothel, but hired rooms out to the soiled doves. He didn't feel right running a business like that. Finally knowing how his business was run, made her love him even more.

Luke had morals despite his upbringing, and it filled her with pride.

Marigold watched as he crossed the floor and swooped up little Elizabeth. "What has Papa told you about touching the Christmas tree?" he asked, his voice gentle.

"Not to touch it." Her bottom lip trembled as her head hung low, and Luke patted Elizabeth's back as he leaned her over his shoulder.

"Don't be upset," he said gently. "Just don't do it. Papa docsn't want it to fall on top of you and hurt you."

She suddenly came up to face him, a grin on her face. "Alright, Papa," she said, then wriggled about until Luke put her back on the floor. She ran into the corner of the room Marigold had set up as a play area and swooped up her favorite rag doll, cuddling it close to her chest.

Marigold came to stand next to him. "We did good," she said quietly.

Luke studied her face. "We certainly did," he said, as he laid his hand across her belly. His arm slid up around her, and he pulled her closer. "I love you so much," he said, kissing her gently. "I'll never stop loving you."

Marigold couldn't stop the tears that slid down her face. She wondered where she'd be right now if *Love Struck* had told her to leave Luke and find someone else.

She shook her head. Luke was her forever love, and she knew deep in her heart that she would never have left him. They would be together for the rest of their lives.

The End

From the Author

Thank you so much for reading my book – I hope you enjoyed it.

I would greatly appreciate you leaving a review where you purchased, even if it is only a one-liner. It helps to have my books more visible!

About the Author

Multi-published, award-winning and bestselling author Cheryl Wright, former secretary, debt collector, account manager, writing coach, and shopping tour hostess, loves reading.

She writes both historical and contemporary western romance, as well as romantic suspense.

She lives in Melbourne, Australia, and is married with two adult children and has six grandchildren. When she's not writing, she can be found in her craft room making greeting cards.

Links:

Website: *http://www.cheryl-wright.com/*

Blog: *http://romance-authors.com/*

Facebook Reader Group:
https://www.facebook.com/groups/cherylwrightauthor/